The Fisherman and His Wife

Illustrated by
LAURINDA SPEAR
based on a tale by
the Brothers Grimm

RIZZOLI
NEW YORK

This book is dedicated to Bernardo, Marisa, Alexander,
Nicholas, Raymond, Harold, and Gabriel
Each of whom was my inspiration.
—LS

First published in the United States of America in 1992 by
Rizzoli International Publications, Inc.
300 Park Avenue South, New York, New York 10010

Library of Congress Cataloging-in-Publication Data

Von dem Fischer und seiner Frau. English
    The fish and the fisherman : a tale / by the Brothers
Grimm ; illustrated by Laurinda Spear.
        p.   cm.
    Translation of: Von dem Fischer und seiner Frau.
    Caption title: The fisherman and his wife.
    Summary: The fisherman's greedy wife is never
satisfied with the wishes granted her by an enchanted
fish.
    ISBN 0-8478-1370-3
    [1. Fairy tales.   2. Folklore—Germany.]   I. Grimm,
Jacob, 1785–1863.   II. Grimm, Wilhelm, 1786–1859.
III. Spear, Laurinda, ill.   IV. Title.   V. Title: Fisherman
and his wife.
PZ8.V886 1992
398.21'0943—dc20
[E]   90-26315
                                                         CIP
                                                         AC

Printed and bound by Oversea Printing Supplies Ltd.,
Singapore

Design by Milton Glaser, Inc.

The Fisherman and His Wife

RIZZOLI
NEW YORK

ONCE UPON A TIME, there was a fisherman who lived with his wife in a brightly painted hut near the sea. Every day he went out fishing. One day, there was a great tug on his line, and he pulled in a large dolphin.

The dolphin said to him, "Oh, fisherman, please let me live. I'm not really a dolphin but a prince under a witch's spell. Please throw me back into the water!"

"There's no need to beg, my good friend. I'm amazed you can talk. Of course I'll let you go." The fisherman cut the line to release the dolphin, then motored back to shore and went home to his wife and child.

"HUSBAND," HIS WIFE ASKED, "you didn't catch anything today?"

"No, I did catch a dolphin, who said he was an enchanted prince, but I threw him back into the sea," replied the fisherman.

"And what did you wish for?" asked his wife. "An enchanted prince must have granted you a wish."

"No," said the fisherman, "I asked for nothing."

"Well, living in this small hut is certainly not the best of lives," said the woman. "You might have wished for a cottage, after all, you did throw him back. He must at least grant you this wish. Go back and ask him. Go at once." The man didn't want to go, but he didn't wish to upset his wife either, and so he returned to the sea to seek the dolphin.

ONCE OUT AT SEA IN HIS BOAT,
the water became green and yellow,
and quiet, and he called out:

> Dolphin, dolphin in the sea,
> Swim close by and speak to me,
> For my wife, sweet Isabil,
> Wills not as I'd have her will.

The dolphin leapt from the water
and asked, "What does she want?"

"I did let you go," said the man,
unable to meet the fish's stare, "so my
wife says I should have wished for
something. She doesn't like to live in a
hut but wishes to have a cottage."

"Return to her," said the dolphin.
"She has it already."

WHEN the man went home,
his wife was sitting on a bench before
the door of a quaint stucco cottage,
the color of spring roses. She took him
by the hand and said, "Look, now isn't
this a great deal better?" In the yard
were hens and ducks and a little garden
with flowers and fruit trees.

"Yes," said her husband, "and now
we will live quite happily."

"We shall see," said his wife.
With that they ate their supper and
went to bed.

E VERYTHING WENT WELL
for a week, then the woman said,
"Husband, this cottage is too small for
us. The dolphin could have made it a bit
larger. Instead, I would like to live in a
stone castle. Go tell the dolphin."

"Wife," replied the fisherman, "the
dolphin has given us this cottage which
suits our needs perfectly. I don't wish to
go back and ask for more; he might
become angry."

"Go, he can do it quite easily. Just
ask him," said the woman.

When the man came to the sea,
the water was dark purple and thick,
and no longer green and yellow, but it
was still quiet. He swam out past the
surf and said:

Dolphin, dolphin in the sea,
Swim close by and speak to me,
For my wife, sweet Isabil,
Wills not as I'd have her will.

"Well, what does she want now?"
asked the dolphin.

"She wants to live in a stone castle."

"Return to her; she has it already."

W HEN he arrived home, the fisherman found a great castle of coral rock and a sandstone tower. The castle was floating on the water, connected to the land by a single drawbridge. His wife ran out to greet him.

"Isn't this wonderful!" exclaimed the woman.

"Yes," replied the man. "Now we have everything we need."

"We shall see," said his wife. With that they ate their supper and went to bed.

JUST BEFORE DAYBREAK, the wife awoke, and from her bed, she saw the countryside lying before her. Her husband was still asleep, so she shook him awake and said, "Get up and look out the window. Wouldn't you wish to be king over all the land that we can see? Go to the dolphin and say you wish to be king."

"But I don't wish to be king," mumbled the man, as he was not quite awake.

"Well, if you don't, I do," said his wife. "Go to the dolphin this instant; I must be king!"

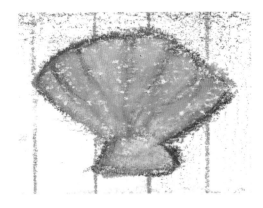

WHEN he came to the sea, it was quite green and dark. The water heaved up from below, and smelled horrible. He called out:

Dolphin, dolphin in the sea,
Swim close by and speak to me,
For my wife, sweet Isabil,
Wills not as I'd have her will.

"Well, what does she want now?" asked the dolphin.

"She wishes to be king," replied the man.

"Return to her; she is king already."

So the man went home and, when he came to the castle, it had become much larger. The main building was five stories high and made of polished pink marble on a golden travertine base. Behind it in a magnificent courtyard were two towers clad in brilliant red and yellow onyx. Completing the courtyard was another wing of polished silver granite. His wife was waiting for him on the fifth floor balcony.

WHEN he entered the hall and stood before her, he said, "And now that you are king, be happy with what you have and wish for nothing more."

"No, husband," said his wife anxiously. "I can't bear it any longer, go to the dolphin. I am king, but I must be emperor!"

"Oh, wife, he can't make you emperor. There are many kings, of which now you are one, but in all these lands there is only one emperor. Therefore, he can't make you emperor."

"Go, at once, for if he can make a king, then he can make an emperor. Go instantly," she commanded, raising her scepter above her head.

The man jogged down to the shore. The sea was purple, black and thick, and began to boil up from below, and a strong wind blew over it, and the man was afraid. But he shouted out:

Dolphin, dolphin in the sea,
Swim close by and speak to me,
For my wife, sweet Isabil,
Wills not as I'd have her will.

"Now what does she want?" asked the dolphin.

"Oh, dolphin," said the man, wringing his hands, "my wife wishes to be emperor."

"Return to her then," said the dolphin. "She is emperor already."

THE MAN ARRIVED where
the castle once stood to discover an
immense palace of polished marble with
eight towers, each made of a different
precious or semi-precious stone: ruby,
jade, emerald, turquoise, amethyst,
coral, silver, and gold. The palace was
twelve stories high. This time his wife
was not outside waiting for him.

THE FISHERMAN ENTERED THE great hall and was led by the guard to the grand dining room. There he found his wife.

"Wife," he asked, "are you emperor now?"

"Yes, I am emperor," she replied.

"Then wife, be content with this."

"We shall see," said the woman. With that they ate their supper and went to bed.

WHEN the sun began to rise, the woman went to the window. She said to herself, "I can order whatever I wish throughout the land, for I alone am emperor. But, I cannot order the sun and moon to rise, nor the stars to appear."

She returned to the bed and said to her husband, "Wake up. Go to the dolphin, for I have another wish to make. I wish to be as God is."

In his horror, the man fell out of their bed. Jumping to his feet he said, "Wife, what are you saying!"

"Husband," said his wife, "if I can't order the sun and moon to rise and the stars to appear but must see the sun and moon rise and the stars appear, I can't bear it. I will never be happy again, unless it is I who commands them." Then she looked at him with such a wretched look on her face, that he shuddered. "Go, husband, go at once; I wish to be as God is."

"Wife," exclaimed the man, "the dolphin cannot do this, go on as you are, you are emperor, let that be enough."

"I can't stand it!" screamed his wife, tearing at her gown. "I can't stand it any longer. You must go, you must!"

So the fisherman ran as fast as he could to the sea, not even waiting for breakfast.

A GREAT STORM was raging over the water, so that he could barely keep the boat afloat. Houses were blown away, trees torn from the ground, and rain fell like arrows from the sky. Mountains trembled and the air reverberated with the crash of thunder. The sea was deep, dark black with waves as high as church steeples. The man cried out, but could not hear his own voice above the tempest that raged about him:

> Dolphin, dolphin in the sea,
> Swim close by and speak to me,
> For my wife, sweet Isabil,
> Wills not as I'd have her will.

"What does she want?" demanded the dolphin.

The man trembled and could barely speak he was so afraid. "She wants to be as God is," he stammered.

"Return to her. She waits for you outside your hut."

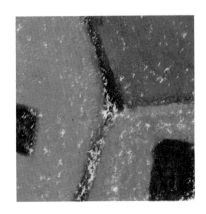

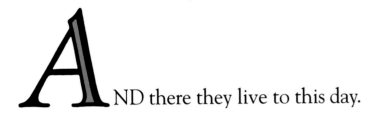ND there they live to this day.

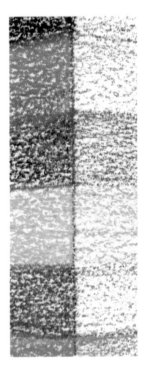

LAURINDA SPEAR *has practiced architecture since 1977 with her husband, Bernardo Fort-Brescia, in their firm, Arquitectonica. The firm is known for having romanticized an architecture for Miami—its work has become the city's hallmark in photography, film, and television. Today, Arquitectonica has expanded its vision and has built works throughout the United States, Europe, and South America. The firm has received a number of awards, among them AIA Honor Awards and Progressive Architecture Design Awards.*

Arquitectonica has literally changed the skyline of Miami. Its projects range from low-income housing, high-rise condominiums, residences, and renovations to office towers, institutional buildings, retail complexes, and hotels.

Ms. Spear graduated from Brown University and received a masters degree in architecture from Columbia University. She was a recipient of the prestigious Rome Prize in Architecture for study at the American Academy in Rome in 1978. She has taught a design studio at the University of Miami and has lectured extensively around the country.

Ms. Spear lives with her six children, ranging in age from one to twelve, in a house near the ocean in Miami. Ever since she was a child, she has loved the sea and especially dolphins.